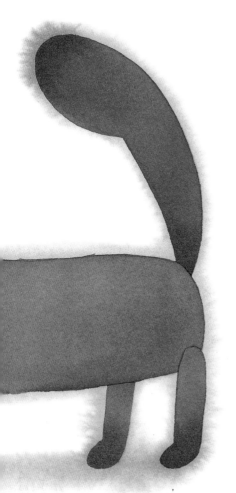

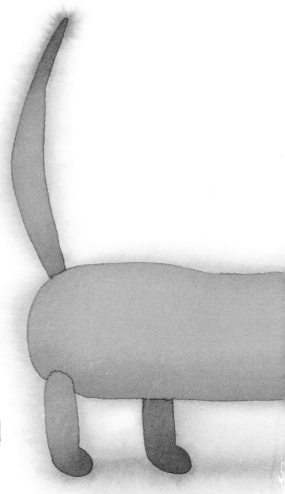

Un gato y un perro

A Cat and a Dog

escrito por Claire Musurel
ilustrado por Bob Kolar

traducido por Andrés Antreasyan

North South

First bilingual edition published in the United States and Canada in 2003 by Ediciones Norte-Sur,
an imprint of NordSüd Verlag AG, CH-8005 Zürich, Switzerland.
Distributed in the United States by NorthSouth Books, Inc., New York 10016.
Spanish text supervised by Sur Editorial Group, Inc..

Library of Congress Cataloging-in-Publicaion Data is available.
Printed in China by Toppan Leefung Printing Limited, Dongguan, April 2013.
ISBN 978-0-7358-1784-5 (bilingual paperback edition) 10 9 8 7

www.northsouth.com

Un gato y un perro vivían en la misma casa.

A cat and a dog lived in the same house.

Pero no eran amigos.

But they were not friends.

GRRR!

GRRR!

Peleaban todo el tiempo,

They fought all the time,

¡Perro torpe!

Clumsy dog!

noche . . .

night . . .

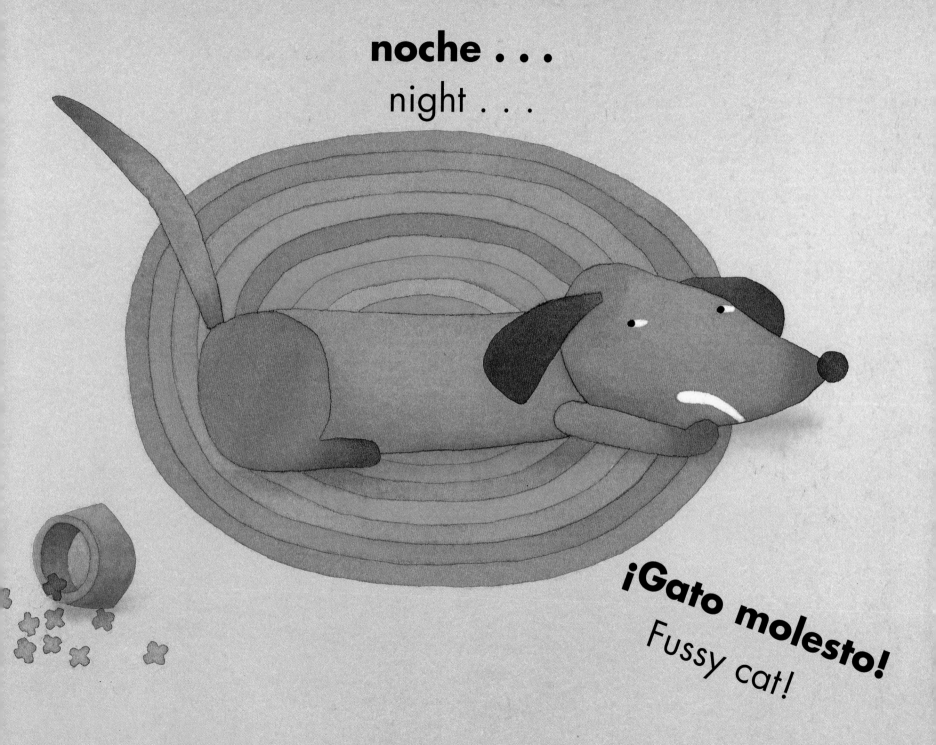

¡Gato molesto!

Fussy cat!

y día.

and day.

¡Perro sucio!

Dirty dog!

¡Gato perezoso!

Lazy cat!

Peleaban por todo,

They fought about everything,

los mejores lugares,

the best spots,

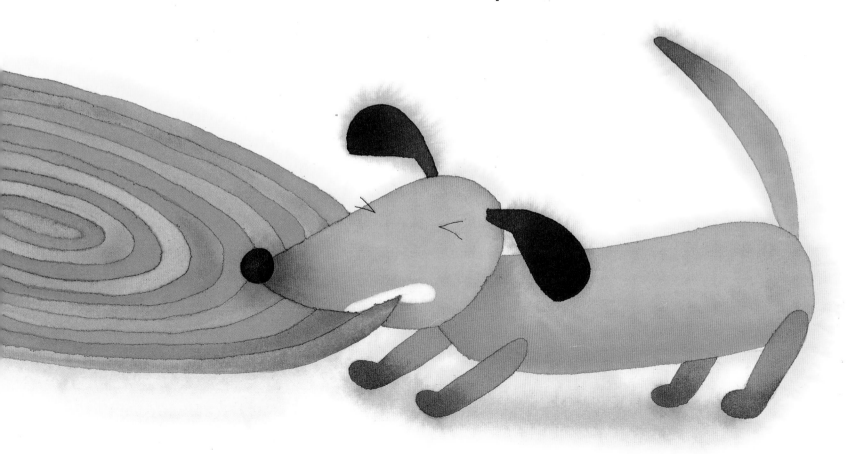

la mejor comida.

the best treats.

Pero más que nada, peleaban por los juguetes.

But most of all, they fought about their toys.

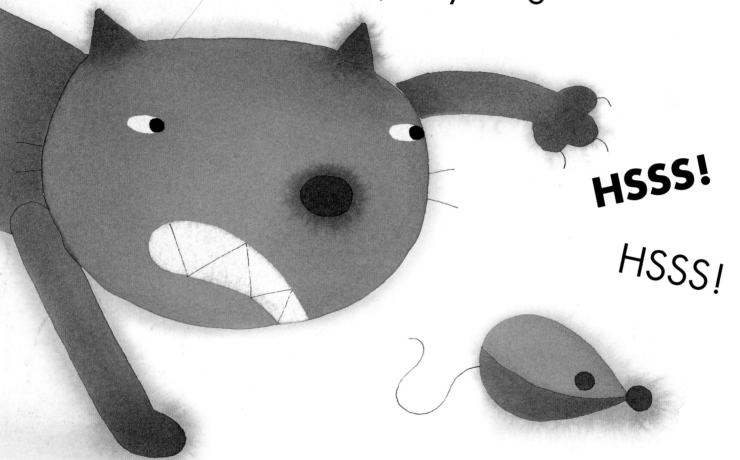

HSSS!

HSSS!

¿Ves estas garras? ¡No te acerques a mi ratoncito!

See these claws? Stay away from my mouse!

GRRR!

GRRR!

¿Ves estos colmillos? ¡No te acerques a mi pelota!

See these fangs? Stay away from my ball!

El gato y el perro jugaban solos.

The cat and the dog played on their own.

Mordisqueando

Chewing

Persiguiendo

Chasing

Rodando

Rolling

Atrapando

Catching

Hasta que un día, pasó algo terrible.

Then one day, something terrible happened.

¡OH, NO!

OH, NO!

No sé nadar.

I can't swim.

¡OH, NO!
OH, NO!

No sé trepar.

I can't climb.

No había absolutamente nada que pudieran hacer.

There was absolutely nothing they could do.

¿Nada?
Nothing?

¡Ya sé!
I know!

¡Yo sé nadar!

I can swim!

¡Toma, Gato!

Here, Cat!

¡Toma, Perro!

Here, Dog!

**Un gato y un perro viven
en la misma casa . . .**

A cat and a dog live
in the same house . . .

y ahora son los mejores amigos.

and now they are the best of friends.